MW00882385

BIGFOOT WAR
Frontier

Bigfoot War: Frontier
Copyright © 2012 Eric S. Brown

First Edition

This book is protected under the copyright laws of the United States of America. Any reproduction or unauthorized use of the material or photographs contained herein is prohibited without the express written permission of the author or artist.

This book is a work of fiction. Names, characters, places, and incidents either are products of the author's imagination or are used fictitiously. Any resemblance to actual events or locales or persons, living or dead, is entirely coincidental.

Edited By: Jason Thacker

Cover Art By: Gary McCluskey

Layout and Design: Jason Thacker

ISBN 10: 1481205013
ISBN 13: 978-1481205016

First Printing: December, 2012

AUTHOR'S NOTE

These events take place prior to those
of Bigfoot War IV.

BIGFOOT WAR: FRONTIER

The sun fell in the sky, sinking ever closer to the mountains in the west. Tall, green grass stretched to the horizon in all directions as Clint and Logan rode towards them. Both men were tired and the day had been a long one. Clint was on edge still expecting to run into a war party of Indians at any moment. When their group had taken shelter at Fort Steel, the soldiers there had warned them that the Indians in these parts were up in arms. Clint was rather attached to his scalp and had no desire for it to be hanging as a trophy on some savage's belt. There had been signs that showed there were indeed Indians around that they had come across earlier in the day but Logan assured him, they had nothing to worry about. Logan was a professional scout and guide who'd seen several wagon trains of folk through this region. Clint didn't doubt Logan's competence but he was keenly aware of his own luck. It always seemed to lean heavily on the bad side of things. Of all the men in the group, somehow Clint had ended up being the one to ride ahead with Logan to make sure the way was clear despite the fact that he was a terrible shot and most of the other men jokingly called him City Slicker. He was a jeweler by trade and this whole experience was rather unsettling to him. If it wasn't for his wife's insistence, he would still be back east right now... but however much he might hate it out here, Clint had to admit there was land to be had and money to be made in the West. They could start over and open a new shop with no threat of the competition that had nearly drove him out of business back home before they had pulled up stakes and headed westward.

"We should make the woods by nightfall," Logan said, spitting a mouthful of tobacco juice into the grass.

Clint looked at Logan, meeting his gaze but said nothing.

"You're still afraid of the Indians aren't ya? Don't be," Logan patted the Winchester resting across his saddle. "I've had run ins with them before. They're hunting soldiers not us. Unless they're really riled up, odds are they'll leave the two of us alone. We're not a big enough of a threat to worry them."

Though he nodded, Clint remained unconvinced. They rode on in silence. As their shadows grew longer and the sky above darker, they reached the woods below the mountain pass just as Logan had predicted they would.

"We'll camp here," Logan informed him, bringing his horse to a stop. "In the morning, we'll start back and fetch the others."

Clint dismounted and tied his horse next to Logan's at the edge of the woods.

"I'll take first watch," Logan said, "You go on and get some rest city boy."

"What about supper?" Clint complained as his stomach growled angrily.

"No fire tonight. Ain't any sense in asking for trouble."

Clint frowned. He had some hardtack tucked away in his saddlebag. It would have to do. Clint dug it out and gnawed on the tough bread as Logan made a show of checking his rifle. He supposed Logan did it to help him rest easier but it didn't help. It only reminded Clint that they were alone and far from any kind of civilization.

Darkness rolled in hard and fast. Sleeping on the ground was something that Clint was getting used to, but that fact still didn't make it comfortable. He lay awake listening to the sounds of the night. As sheer exhaustion began to claim him and his eyes drooped closed, an inhuman cry echoed among the trees. Clint bolt upright, his hand grabbing the rifle that rested in the grass beside him.

Logan was awake and alert, his own eyes scanning the tree line.

"What was that?" Clint demanded.

"Don't rightly know," Logan admitted. The night was a clear one and the stars above gave them enough light to see a little. Something moved in the woods not far from the camp.

"Whatever it is, it's big," Logan grunted. "That's for sure."

The thing in the woods shrieked again. The cry was earsplitting and filled with anger.

"A bear maybe?" Clint asked.

Logan laughed despite their situation and shook his head. "Ain't no bear. You heard that didn't you? Almost sounded like a man."

Clint saw Logan gave him a quick glance as he added, "Ain't no Indian either. You just keep that rifle in your hands and ready. Whatever it is, if it comes along in this direction, we'll fill it so full of bullets it won't be recognizable anyway."

Thinking he heard a trace of fear in Logan's voice, Clint nearly wet himself. If whatever the thing was could rattle someone as rough and experienced as Logan, they could be in real trouble. Then Clint saw it. Logan must have seen the beast too because Clint heard him whisper, "Lord in Heaven..."

The beast stood over nine feet tall. Its yellow eyes shined like a cat's in the darkness of the trees. Its arms were thick with muscles, covered in mangy hair like the rest of its body, and were much longer than a man's as they dangled at its sides. The beast made no move towards them. It merely watched them as if waiting for them to make the first move. Sweat born of fear beaded on Clint's forehead and dripped into his eyes. Keeping his Winchester pointed at the beast, he quickly wiped the sweat away with the backside of his other hand. Logan shouldered his rifle and Clint saw him taking aim at the beast.

Somehow the thing must have known what a rifle was. It roared and charged forward as Logan's finger squeezed the trigger. The Winchester cracked. Clint saw Logan's shot smack into the beast's chest but the bullet didn't even slow the monster down. If the shot hurt the beast at all, it gave no sign of it. Logan was working his rifle's lever to chamber another round as the beast plowed into him. One of the beast's large hands grabbed Logan. Its fingers sunk deep into his flesh, digging into his ribs, as Logan screamed. The beast lifted Logan effortlessly from the ground by the fingers buried inside him. Logan's screams became a blood clogged gargle as the beast flung him into the trunk of a nearby tree. Clint heard the crunching sound of breaking bones as Logan's body smashed into the trunk and blood splattered into the night air. The beast turned to face him as Clint opened fire. He aimed for the beast's head and missed. The beast marched slowly towards him showing no fear of the weapon in his hands. It was as if it somehow sensed his own fear and didn't see him as a threat despite the rifle. Clint chambered another round and fired again. This time his shot smacked into the beast's shoulder. The beast drew ever closer to where he stood as he worked the Winchester's lever a third time. He prayed a silent prayer as he took aim and squeezed the trigger again. The beast's left eye exploded in a spray of red tinted pulp and blood. The monster shrieked like a wounded cat and staggered a few steps backwards. It recovered quickly, shaking its head about and flinging blood then gave a deep, guttural growl of pure rage. Clint screamed as it lunged at him with superhuman speed. The last thing he ever saw was a giant, hair covered fist coming towards his head.

Ray sat in the saddle of his horse, leaning slightly forward, as he watched camp being broken. Men, women, and children scurried about their wagons getting ready for another long, hard day on the move. The group wasn't overly large, numbering around fifty or sixty travelers total. There were nearly twenty wagons in the train and usually four other riders like himself who kept guard and acted as scouts surrounding them at any given time. Ray wasn't very good with people unless he had to be and thus far had only bothered to get know a few of his fellow travelers. They all shared one thing in common, the desire to start over and seek a brighter future. What that future might be though varied on a case by case basis. Some looked westward for gold, others land, still others he supposed just for the adventure and being able to brag about having made the journey. For himself, it was none of those things. Ray Warren, as he called himself now, just wanted to stay free and keep breathing. There had been trouble back east that he needed to escape and for him like some of the others the West was his only hope of another chance, a place where he wouldn't have to keep looking over his shoulder for the bullet in the back that he deserved.

No one knew why Logan and the city fellow had never returned but after giving them two extra days in which to do so beyond their appointed time, a vote had been taken and the wagons rolled on. Tension was running high and no one wanted to admit that the Indians rumored to be on the warpath in the area might have gotten them. Ray hadn't known either of the two men well, but his gut told him Indians weren't the reason they were missing. From what he had seen of Logan, that man wasn't the sort who took chances or got caught off guard easily. The only way Indians would have gotten him was if the city slicker did something truly stupid or there were so many of the Indians, no single man could have stood against them and lived. Ray had spoken up and said just that when the others had taken their vote, but the call of the West was too strong no matter what might be waiting on them out there.

Ray looked up as David came riding over to join him.

"Morning," David tipped his hat as he drew up his horse beside Ray's.

Ray nodded at him.

"Weren't you on the night watch?" David asked.

Ray shrugged. "Don't matter none. I ain't tired yet."

David frowned at him. Ray knew he meant well but something about David just rubbed him the wrong way. David was one of those confident, overly pleasant folks you either just loved or hated. That was how he had ended up in charge of the wagon train, Ray's opinion being in the minority. David had been a law man back east and you could see it in how he carried himself and the shiny Colt holstered on his belt.

"You should get some rest," David urged him. "Earl can take your place. That old boy snored up a storm last night."

Ray grunted. "Done told ya, I'm fine."

David appeared offended but his annoying smile stayed on his lips. "Suit yourself then, but I need everybody on lookout especially sharp today. We're far enough away from Fort Steel now that we're really on our own ya know? If any Indians come calling, we need to be ready for them."

That said, David tugged on his horse's reins, turning it about and headed to where the wagons were busy forming up to roll out. Ray watched him go, gritting his teeth at the frustration of dealing with the former law man and forced himself to calm down.

"Mama!" Jocie called. "Vincent's doing it again!"

Darlene sighed sitting her handful of breakfast dishes into the back of their wagon and then snapped, "Vincent Edward Jenkins! You leave your sister alone this instant!"

Darlene didn't even have to glance over her shoulder to know what was going on but sure enough when she turned, Vincent was sticking his tongue out and making horrid faces at Jocie. Vincent stopped and went pale, struck by the anger in her voice. She marched over to him and stood with her hands on her hips. "Young man don't you have work to do?"

"Yes, ma'am?" Vincent answered. As he moved passed her and climbed into the wagon where Jocie had already disappeared to, Darlene sighed again, shaking her head. There were problems aplenty in her life without her eleven year old son adding to them. Her husband had died of the Pox last year, leaving her with debts that she couldn't possibly pay. No one had stepped up to help her. Her husband had been a surly man, too attached to the bottle for his own good or theirs. Not even the pastor of the local church seemed to care about their plight. Darlene cried when the bank took the farm but tears didn't change the fact that she had children to care for and feed.

By chance, she had heard of the free land being offered in the West and their course was set. She worked the saloon and the streets for a month, selling off everything they had left too in order to buy the wagon and horses for this journey. Many of the men making the journey with them had expressed the wrong kind of interest in her, but Darlene swore her "street" days were over. Never again would she give herself away like that unless it was to a man she loved. David, Ray, and Earl did their best to keep those men under control and she was thankful for it. Even so, Darlene carried a concealed knife at all times and there was a double barrel shotgun hidden in the wagon if it came to it. The weapon lay buried among the stacks of their supplies and meager belongings, underneath the wagon's cover. She wasn't ready for a new husband yet, but Earl had caught her eye anyway. The big man was so compassionate and gentle despite his gruff appearance and size. She wondered what her life would have been like if she had met him before the deadbeat she had married. Jerry, her late husband, had deserved to get the Pox and part of her was truly glad he was dead and rotting in the dirt. Darlene got Vincent settled in the back of the wagon and raced up front to be ready for when David gave the signal to get moving.

Jocie rode shotgun beside her. Darlene couldn't help but smile as she saw Jocie's youthful, innocent eyes taking in the majesty of the landscape around them. Jocie turned her head to meet her with a smile as she climbed up to take the reins of the horses.

"We're on our way Mom," Jocie said.

Darlene nodded trying to see their situation as her excited and hopeful daughter did.

"You bet we are baby," Darlene smiled back at her. "You bet we are."

Pastor Page missed the fields of his farm and his congregation in North Carolina. The faithful members of his church had been like family to him. The Lord had worked wonders in the small town he had called home. Though there were still places where the more hardened men of the little community gathered to drink, there was no proper saloon. There were no dancing girls being exploited and abused. The greatest crimes were nothing more than mere disagreements and the residents kept their guns holstered. Crops grew full and green. There was very little sickness. Everyone helped one another and prayed together with him come Sunday morning. That valley among the hills had been so blessed that when the Lord called upon him to travel west to continue his witness to new flocks, Pastor Page did all he could to quiet that voice inside him. But no one could ignore the will of God forever. Pastor Page gave his farm to the town and surrendered his church to a younger man of God the Lord had sent to the town. After many a tearful goodbye, he had set out for the West with nothing more than the clothes on his back, the Bible in his hands, and his faith. Now here he was, like the disciples of old, allowing God to use him as the Lord saw fit. He had no wagon or even a horse of his own but the Lord had provided his way. The Watkins' took him in and he became a part of their family on this long and perilous journey. He sat on the front the wagon, riding next to John. Angie and their daughter, Grace, rode in the wagon's rear beneath its cover. The sun was hot and bright in the sky above and a thick sea of green covered the ground around the slow moving wagon train in every direction as the horses strained and the wheels turned.

"What you reckon happened to Logan and that there city fellow?" John asked. "You think them Indians really got them?"

Pastor Page shrugged. "If the Lord had meant us to know, we would," he answered in a gentle tone.

"Don't suppose it matters," John nodded. "It's pretty clear there ain't none of us here willing to turn back regardless of whatever lies ahead of us."

"I suppose you're right," Pastor Page agreed. The pastor was a large and tough built man. Before he had heard the Lord's call and took to preaching the word, he had been a farmer like his father before him. Even after the Lord blessed him with his own church, Pastor Page had kept on farming just the same during his spare time. He as a firm believer that hard work and toil were good for the soul. All those years spent in the fields showed on his hands, tanned skin, and in his muscles. Of the men in the wagon train only Earl was bigger but it was impossible to say who was stronger. Pastor Page hoped there would never be an occasion to find out either. Like all men who lived off the land in this age, he was no stranger to violence. He never sought it out, but it had found him in his life more than once. There were times he had been forced to raise a hand to defend a battered wife or an abused child. Very few people he met ever took him for a man of God until they heard him speak and saw the well-worn Bible he rarely put down clutched tightly in his hands.

John interrupted his thoughts again. "Pastor, if those Indians do come for us, can I count on you to stand with me? I mean, I know killing is a sin and all but..."

Pastor Page stared at John. A moment of silence passed between them. "I give you my word John; I will do all I can to keep your family safe."

John seemed to grow calmer and smiled. "Thank you, Pastor. That means a lot to me."

Pastor Page nodded and looked up at the sky full of rolling white clouds above them. The Lord has a plan, he thought, and his will be done in all things.

Earl held the reins of the head wagon in his hands and drove the horses on as Ray rode over to keep pace beside him.

"You see'em?" Ray asked.

"What?" Earl grunted.

"Them mountains up ahead don't look too friendly."

Earl laughed, long and loud. "Don't tell me the great Ray Warren is getting spooked?"

Ray frowned. "Didn't say that," he answered firmly. "I was just pointing out that we could still go around them. Ain't too late ya know? That pass ain't the only way west."

Earl shook his head, his long black beard scraping at his shirt as he moved. "No but that pass is the shortest route. I sat beside you at the meeting remember? I know you would rather go another way but that ain't what we decided is it?"

Ray spat in the grass. "Don't mean it was the right decision. Out here on the plain, we're safer. Nothing gonna sneak up on us out here. We'd see them Indians coming a long way off. In those woods..."

"What you want me to do about it Ray?" Earl asked. "David's in charge and everybody else agreed that pass was the right choice."

Ray wondered what he had expected to gain by bringing it all up to Earl again. David was the only one who could call another meeting, and that hardheaded idiot, he had set his course. There was no reasoning with him and

Ray knew it. Men like David didn't back down unless it suited them, and right now David was riding high. Everyone wanted this journey over with as quick as it could be and for all its dangers the trail through the mountains and the woods around them offered exactly that. Cutting through the pass would shave days, if not a full week off their journey west. "Sorry I bothered you," Ray said to Earl. "I guess I just had to say my piece out loud one more time."

"Trust me, Ray, I hear ya, but there ain't nothing to be worried about in them woods that we can't handle. As long as the wagons can make it through without problems, this is the road to take."

Ray turned in his saddle and started to ride off and get back to a better position in which to keep an eye out for trouble, but Earl called to him.

"Hey Ray! Got something I been meaning to ask you as long as you're here."

Ray raised an eyebrow. "What ya need, Earl?"

Earl motioned for him to ride closer to the wagon. Ray did so as Earl leaned over to him. "I been thinking, Ray. I've seen that Darlene lady giving me the eye. She ain't bad looking either. You think..."

Ray's lips parted in an amused grin. "Earl, are you asking me what I think you're asking?"

The big man's cheeks went red. "Look, I ain't never been good with women. I just wanted to know if you've seen her looking at me too or is it all in my head? I been alone a long time, Ray. I don't want to go making a fool of myself in front of everybody. You understand?"

Ray struggled not to laugh. Earl could likely break him in half without much effort, but the big man was scared to death of a little, redheaded woman from the south. That was how it worked with women though wasn't it? A man could never be sure of anything with them unless they carved it into stone right in front of their face. "She sure doesn't seem to not like you, Earl. Man up and make the first move if you want to court her. You'll never know how she felt one way or the other if you don't.

Earl sighed and looked resigned to his fate. "Guess you're right, Ray. Some things you just gotta go for if you want them."

"I'd rightly agree with that," Bentley said poking his head out of the wagon's interior.

"Thought you were asleep," Earl huffed.

"I was," the spry little Irish man grinned. "But hushed conversations have a way of catching my interest. I just can't resist them."

Earl appeared ready to take Bentley by the throat and snap his neck. Bentley must have seen the anger burning in the big man's eyes because he quickly added, "Aye. It's none of me business, but none the less I couldn't help but overhear. I assure you, Earl, there's no shame in seeking a fine lass like that one's hand, if you take my meaning, and I too have sought out the council of others in days gone by before making such a move."

Ray watched Earl glare at the little Irish man. "Don't you worry about Bentley there, Earl," Ray said hoping Earl wasn't going to let his temper get the best of him. "He's got secrets of his own."

"Mighty right I do," Bentley added. "And even if I didn't, I am no fool sir. If the lass is to hear of your passionate intentions, it shall not be from me."

Ray relaxed as he saw Earl shift in his seat and turn his attention back to the horses in front of the wagon.

"Just talk to her, Earl. Tell her how you feel," Ray urged the big man. "What's the worst that can happen?"

Snell puffed on a hand rolled cigarette as he rode across the plain. Normally he didn't take jobs like this one. He preferred hunting murders and rapists but the money was just too good to pass up. The ivory butts of matching Colt revolvers protruded from the tops of the holsters on his hips and a Winchester was strapped to his back over the sheath of a strangely shaped sword beneath it. A double barrel shotgun was sheathed on the saddle of his horse and each of his boots held a razor sharp knife. His skin was leathery and his eyes hard. The tip of a long, ugly scar that ran the length of his arm from elbow to wrist poked out from underneath the right sleeve of his shirt. Snell enjoyed jobs that had the dead or alive option. Killing was the only thing he had ever shown a talent for and he had honed that talent until he had become a master of death. The good Lord blessed him with hands like lightning and a sharp mind. This job however was of the peculiar sort. He wasn't even after a man, but rather what the man had stolen. Not only that, he wasn't working for the law or some slighted cattle lord with deep pockets this go round, but the blasted United States Army. He had no use for government and even less for snotty, pampered officers. But the money they were paying him by the time this job was done, he would be able to retire for the rest of his life if he chose to. Whatever this Bentley fellow had stolen from them was surely unique and not the kind of thing you wanted folks at large to know about. There were no posters of the Irish man plastered around his usual haunts. The whole job was very hush, hush. Colonel Hipps had sought him out personally for this gig. Snell's reputation was that of a man who got the job done no matter the cost, and folks said he could be trusted to be discrete when needed. It all stunk of treason and danger, but Snell thrived on death, and a bit of blood did one good. There was a chance the army would try to double cross him when he returned the prototype, whatever in tarnation it was, but if he couldn't handle a power drunk fool like the colonel, he didn't need to be in this line of work anyway. The colonel had assured him he would know exactly what he needed to bring back when he found Bentley and the thing, but Snell still didn't like being in the dark about his goal. That kind of vagueness, no matter the reason, could lead to failure and Snell prided himself on the fact that he had never taken a job he hadn't completed to satisfaction before. The man, Bentley, was a bookworm and an inventor. If the colonel had told the truth, he would be no threat. That would be no sport at all, taking his life if it came to that. Snell expected it would too. If the man had the stones to steal from the military, Snell figured he wasn't about to just hand over his invention. Reclaiming the prototype would be child's play if he could catch up to the Irish man. Snell knew he was on the right trail though. The soldiers at Fort Steel had verified that Bentley was part of the wagon train he was following. Bentley opting to flee west made sense. The further the Irish man got from the capital's reach, the better off he would be. A man could lose himself in the West and disappear forever if he tried hard enough. Snell had no intention of letting Bentley make it west though. The wagon train was headed for what the Indians called, The Devil's Pass. One man moving alone was far faster than any group, and he would catch them there. Of that, he was sure. If Bentley had made friends among his traveling companions who were willing to stand up for him, well, he could handle that too.

David raised a hand in the air, stopping the line of wagons behind him. They had reached the edge of the woods around the mountains known as the Devil's Pass. The trail they were on continued into the trees like a road. For all that the stories claimed that the Indians kept away from this place, someone still traveled through these parts or had in days gone by. He could tell at a glance that the trail would be rough on the wagons but not impossible for them to make it over. Once they were on it, circling the wagons would no longer be an option. The trail was barely large enough for a wagon with a rider on each side of it to pass through. Even having two wagons travel side by side wouldn't be possible on it. The blasted thing was just too narrow. The trees and brush were thick on both sides of the trail and there would be ample opportunity for ambushers, Indian or otherwise, to creep upon them, especially after darkness fell. Still, even with its roughness, they would be over the trail and through the mountains in less than two days.

David could see and understand why Ray and a few others were so opposed to taking this trail, but he knew if the group was careful and stayed on guard, they would be all right. David looked back over his shoulder at Earl on the lead wagon. The big man was looking passed him at the trail with a scowl on his face.

"You ready?" David called back to him. "Or should we make camp here for the night?"

"Your call," Earl yelled. "Got a couple of hours left until sundown."

David nodded, reminding himself he was in charge here. "Right," he shouted "Let's press on. Watch out for those bumps on the trail though. I don't want to be stopping for busted wheels or broken axles."

Earl's scowl grew darker. "You got it boss man," Earl answered him. "I'll pass the word back to the others."

David tipped the brim of his hat lower against the rays of the sun and stared into the woods. The gnarled, reaching branches of the trees lining the trail gave him an uneasy feeling he couldn't quite explain or put a finger on. Beyond the state of the trail and how hard it would be on the wagons, there was nothing here to give him pause, but despite himself and his continued confidence, something did. He shrugged off the uneasy feeling and gave the signal for the wagons to get moving again as he dismounted and walked his horse on into the trees ahead of them, his Winchester in one hand, the horse's reigns in the other.

Rain lay on her belly in the tall grass watching the crazy white men enter the woods. She was silent and perfectly still. None of them could know she was there. The oneness of her people with the land was legendary and it served her well now. She had left her tribe as they once more went to war with the blue coats and came here to be alone. Not even the bravest warriors dared to venture too near these mountains and thus she had hoped no one would find her here. She wanted to be alone and have time to heal from her shame and to avoid the blood that her people sought from those who came into their lands and claimed them as their own. These white men put her in a difficult position for they would surely disturb those who lived among the trees of these woods. If she did not warn them, they all would die. Rain owed them nothing other than hatred that she couldn't bring herself to feel, but even if she let them die, she would be forced to leave as those in the trees would come for her as well in their fury. If she left and her people stumbled upon her, she would be forced back into the life of a squaw and a shamed one at that. If she stayed, her only hope was to join the white men and their wagons. Perhaps their guns and numbers would see at least some of them through the pass and her with them. She clinched her hands in anger so tightly that her nails dug into the flesh of palms. With a grunt, she shoved herself to her feet and walked, openly, towards the wagon train. One of the wagon train's riders spotted her at once. She braced herself half expecting a rifle bullet to cut her down, but continued to walk forward. The rider's expression was one of utter shock and his rifle rose to point at her, but just as quickly, the man on the horse lowered it as he saw she was alone. "Don't you move!" he warned her.

Rain knew enough English to understand his words and stopped in her tracks. She waited as he wheeled his horse about and rode up to her. The man wore a wide brimmed hat and a black, loose shirt spotted with damp patches of sweat from the heat of the day. He looked to be near the age of thirty or not much beyond it. His features were angular and his face bird like. The man was thin and clean shaven. Though his rifle was lowered, she could feel the potential for violence within him and his ability to deliver it if needed. He looked her up and down with an appraising glance.

"Are you alone?" he asked.

Rain gave a quick, sharp nod.

"You speak English?"

"Yes," Rain answered. "I learned from traders and travelers as have most of my people."

"What's your name?"

"In your tongue I would be called Rain."

The man smiled. "My name is Ray Warren and you're dang lucky it was me you pulled that come out of nowhere bit on. David over there would have shot you dead."

Ray gestured at another rider approaching them for the trees. The rider reached them as the last of the wagons disappeared, following the trail, into the woods.

"Who's she?" David asked.

"Says her name's Rain and that she's alone."

David snorted. "You're alone? Way out here by yourself?"

"I believe her," Ray said. "See that scar on her cheek?"

Rain was stunned by Ray's words. How could he possibly know what her scar meant?

"So?" David demanded.

"Trust me," Ray gave him a stern look. "She's alone."

"Yes," Rain said, "I was until you came."

"She speaks English?" David started but Ray ignored him, his attention focused on her.

"What do you want Rain?" Ray asked her.

"To live," she answered. "I suspect it is already too late to run. I want to come with you."

"Run?" Ray repeated the word. "Run from what?"

Rain stayed silent. The white men would not believe her even if she told them the truth. She took a breath and stood firm. "May I come with you?"

"No!" David said and spat onto the ground near her. "You go on now before there's trouble and tell your people we're ready for them if they're planning on trying anything. You understand?"

"Wait," Ray spoke up. "You can come with me if you want. I don't have a wagon or anything more than you see right now but you're welcome to share it."

Ray leaned down and offered his hand to her. Rain took it as he hoisted her into the saddle behind him. She could see David, who looked on the verge of bursting with anger.

"You can't do that," he challenged Ray. "You're endangering us all. I'll not stand for it."

Rain saw Ray glare at him.

"You ain't the law, David. This is my horse and if she wants to ride with me, she can."

Rain noticed the fingers of Ray's right hand brush the butt of the pistol holstered on his belt.

David went pale. "Mr. Warren, this is far from over."

David turned his horse around and rode on to catch up to the wagons.

"I'd tell you that you get used to him but I'd be lying," Ray laughed. Dark clouds were rolling in from the east. Ray nodded at them. "Looks like we could have a storm coming."

"Yes," Rain said quietly. "It is."

✳ ✳ ✳

As darkness blotted out the light and night fell over the trail, the wagons came to a halt. The members of the wagon train hurried to get fires going for supper and the night before the rains came. Ray didn't regret his choice to bring Rain along with them but he knew there would be Hell to pay for it as soon as David got a chance to convince the others that she'd bring trouble down on them.

There was no point in having riders on

lookout along the trail. Even if one did manage to navigate their way among the trees on horseback in the darkness, one wouldn't be able to see any better through the woods than guards posted on the wagons themselves, riding shotgun. As thus, Ray had some free time and he took Rain to Earl's wagon to introduce her to the big man.

"This here fellow's Earl. He's a friend of mine. And that red haired gent in the bowler cap is Mr. Bentley."

"Hello," Rain said in a timid voice that didn't suit her appearance.

"Nice to meet you," Earl nodded at her.

"My sincere pleasure as well," Bentley smiled at Rain. "Might I inquire as to what brings us the honor of your company?"

"Bentley," Ray warned.

"No," Rain said, "You have a right to know though I doubt you will believe me."

"You don't have to tell us anything Rain," Ray moved closer to her. "I know what that scar means. That's enough for me."

"My shame brought me to these woods but it is not why I came to you. Your being here is wrong. Death will come for us all this night and I need your guns to have any hope of seeing the dawn."

"Why?" Ray asked. "Is David right? Are your people planning to attack us?"

Rain shook her head. "My people know better than to come here unlike you. These woods... they are not empty. Beasts live here among the trees. It is they who you need to fear, not my people."

"I don't understand," Ray said.

"This is their home and you have entered it. The beasts allow no one here. They will break your bones and drink their marrow before the sun rises unless we are able to fight them off."

"She been smoking the peace pipe a bit much?" Earl chuckled.

"Ssshhh..." Bentley waved at the big man. "What kind of beasts are you talking about ma'am?"

"That's enough," Ray silenced them all. He was going to have enough trouble with David and the others over Rain's presence without her spreading crazy stories. "Bentley, get us some coffee brewing on that fire already. I'll take first watch. Earl, you can go take care of that business we were discussing if you want. And Rain, I respect your people's beliefs, but we ain't got time for stories right now. We all need rest for tomorrow. It'll be rough going on this trail. You can bet we'll see at least one broken axle before the day is through."

Ray watched Rain frown at him but she shut her mouth and set about finding a place to sleep on the ground, close to the fire. Bentley offered her his bedroll in the wagon's rear, but she declined. Ray settled in, sitting by the fire, his Winchester across his knees, and his back against the side of the wagon. His gaze stayed fixed on the trees.

✷ ✷ ✷

Earl left the others, heading down the line of wagons on the trail towards Darlene's. His hands were sweaty and his heart pounded like a hammer against his ribs. Each hello to those he passed on the way was painful. In his mind, they all knew where he was going and why. He thanked God Darlene's wagon was only three back from his own. The first two wagons between him and hers belonged to families he didn't know very well, The Hamlins and the Powells. The fourth wagon however belonged to the Watkins' and the southern pastor they had taken in. There was no escaping them with just a simple hello. John Watkins and the Pastor sat at their fire as Angie worked at mending a hole in the wagon's cover with a sewing needle and thread. Grace was nowhere to be seen. Earl imagined the Watkins' girl had been sent on to bed and slumbered in the back of the wagon. John saw him coming and burst into a smile, getting to his feet to meet him.

"Earl," John said, extending his hand. "What brings you by?"

The pastor got to his feet as well, watching them. Earl wiped his sweaty palm on the leg of his pants and clasped John's hand firmly. Earl nodded in greeting at the pastor then cleared his throat. "Well John, I was actually on my way to check in on someone and make sure they're doing all right."

Angie must have heard him because she

came towards the fire. "There any reason things shouldn't be?" She asked.

"No," Earl shook his head, "Not at all Mrs. Watkins."

Earl was close to David and Ray, the wagon train's leader and its main lookout. Most folks knew that and often picked at him for information on how they were all really faring out here. If something was wrong, odds were Earl would be among the first to know.

Angie looked relieved. "Good," she said quietly. "I am glad to hear it. These woods…"

John cut in, "Guess everyone's sort of on edge, Earl. You'll have to forgive us."

"It ain't nothing," Earl tried to smile but his nerves made it a lopsided effort. "I got to be getting on though. David will have us all rolling out at the crack of dawn."

Having excused himself, Earl continued on into Darlene's camp around her wagon. Like the others, she had a fire burning. She sat near it watching its flames spit embers onto the night breeze. Her kids were likely asleep as he didn't see them anywhere. She looked up at him as he walked closer, her green eyes only made brighter by the fire's light.

"Evening ma'am," Earl managed to say without his voice cracking like a school boy's. Darlene stared at him for a moment before she spoke.

"Dang it Earl, you big oaf. Can't you men ever just leave things as they are?"

Earl's hopes died inside him at her words. "Darlene…" He started but she cut him off.

"You're a good man, Earl, but the truth of things is that I'm not ready for another relationship yet."

Tears formed in the corners of her eyes. "Everything is so hard right now and I have children to look after. I can't do this. I'm sorry."

Earl shifted on his feet, unsure of what to do. "I'm sorry, Darlene," he said, "I didn't mean to..."

"Shut up, Earl. It's not your fault. I like you too, but this just can't happen yet."

Both of them were silent as the fire continued to pop and crackle between them.

"You had best be getting back to your wagon, Earl. It's late."

Earl nodded reluctantly and turned to walk away from her as something in the dark of the woods surrounding the trail roared. Darlene's eyes went wide with fear.

"What the Hell was that?" she said, hopping to her feet.

✳ ✳ ✳

John Watkins grabbed up his rifle as he heard the roar. Never in his life had he heard such a noise. It sounded almost like a man, but it clearly wasn't. It was too deep and too feral. Pastor Page lifted a thick piece of burning wood from the fire and held it like a torch. Whatever was out there was closer to their wagon than it was any of the others. Angie put herself between the trees and the wagon where Grace was sleeping as John glanced at Pastor Page.

"Any idea what that might have been?"

The pastor shook his head. David and one of the men who normally served as a lookout for the wagon train came riding up to their camp.

"Come on," David ordered them as he climbed off his horse and levered a round into the chamber of his rifle. "Anything that can make a noise like that probably ain't too friendly."

John stared at him in disbelief. "You want to go out there after it? In the dark?"

"Would you rather wait here for it to come after your wife and girl?" David asked then said, "Pastor, you got that torch, so you go first. The rest of us will follow you and keep you covered."

Pastor Page didn't seem too happy with David's telling him to take the lead, but he did it anyway.

"Tim, you stay here with the women folk," David told the man who had rode up with him as he moved to follow the pastor, side by side with John. The men hadn't even reached the trees when the monster came barreling out of the woods into the light of the fire.

"Lord protect me!" Pastor Page wailed.

The beast stood ten feet tall, all hair, muscle, and rage. Its yellow eyes burned in the night. Pastor Page swung his makeshift torch at it as he had no other weapon. Embers flew as the piece of wood broke against the thick muscle of the beast's right arm. It brushed the pastor from its path, sending the man of God rolling through the grass as John and the others opened up on it.

John's first hurried shot grazed the thing's cheek, drawing blood as David and Tim's Colts boomed over and over in rapid succession. Tiny dots of red spotted the beast's chest and arms where their bullets hammered into it, but John could see that the rounds weren't getting any real penetration. The thing's muscles and hide were just too thick. All they were doing was making the creature more angry than it already was. It stomped its way towards them, ignoring John even as he managed a second shot that caught the beast in its side. David and Tom's Colts clicked empty as gun smoke hung in the air and the beast plowed into them. One of its massive hands enveloped David's head and popped it like a rotten melon.

John watched Tim screaming and trying to reload as David's blood sprayed over him. Tim dropped his Colt and turned to run, but the beast snatched him up from behind, sinking fingers deep into the flesh of back as it lifted him above its head. John fired a third shot, still with no real effect, as the beast ripped Tim into two pieces along his stomach and tossed Tim's two halves, leaking bowels and red slicked entrails, in different directions.

By now, the sound of the battle and gunfire had drawn folks from all along the line of wagons to John's camp. Earl, Darlene, and Ray had been the first to arrive. Earl and Darlene were already nearby and Ray came running like a bat out of Hell. Darlene carried a double barrel shotgun in her hands and Earl and Ray had their pistols drawn.

As the beast, its hair slicked by Tim's blood, whirled on John, Darlene stepped up beside him and emptied her double barrel point blank into its face. The monster roared, blood pouring from its cheeks and gums, as it staggered backwards.

"Aim for its eyes and throat!" Ray yelled.

Both Ray and Earl fired several rounds into the beast as it recovered from Darlene's blast. One of Ray's shots got lucky and sank deep into the flesh between its chin and chest. The beast slapped a hand over the wound cutting off the geyser of blood spewing out of it. Earl charged the beast.

"Die you son of a..." Earl yelled as he closed in on it emptying the final three shots of his pistol into the monster's forehead. With a whimpering cry, the beast collapsed to one knee. Even so, it was nearly as tall as Ray. It backhanded Earl knocking the big man away from it. Earl was sent flying six feet to flop to the ground near the fire in front of John's wagon.

The beast opened its mouth to roar again. As it did, Ray stepped forward and put a bullet into the roof of its mouth. It snapped its jaws closed as blood leaked from the sides of its closed lips. The beast fell over to lay still in the grass. John started to lower his rifle but Ray shouted "Uh Uh! Let's make damn sure that thing's dead. Don't want it getting up again!"

John jerked his rifle back to his shoulder and added his fire to that of the others. The beast's body twitched and spasmed beneath their combined fire.

"Hold up!" Ray ordered at last. The gunfire fell silent. Ray walked up to the beast's bleeding form and pressed the barrel of his Colt to its skull. John watched him pull the trigger and the blood fly as the bullet broke through already damaged bone. Ray turned and nodded at him and the other men.

"It's done," Ray said.

"Sure," John heard himself say, "but what the Hell is it?"

Ray squatted by the thing's corpse. "Danged if I know but it sure stinks to high heavens."

"That thing walked on two legs like a man," someone in the crowd around them said.

"It's a demon. A demon from Hell," someone else shouted.

John was impressed at how quickly Ray took charge of the situation as he stood. "Don't matter what it was. It's dead folks."

John saw Darlene tending to Earl. The big man still hadn't gotten up from where the creature had knocked him. Earl was clutching the side of his chest with a grimace on his face. No doubt the thing's blow had broken some of his ribs. Then John suddenly remembered Pastor Page.

"I'm okay," Pastor Page said as John spun around at the sound of his voice. "Though I suppose this will still be hurting in the morning." Pastor Page lifted his shirt to show John a large bruise that covered his left side where the creature's hand had shoved him.

John cocked his head, eying the bruise. "Yep, I reckon' so," he agreed, thankful the pastor wasn't hurt worse. "Is that thing really a demon?"

Pastor Page shook his head. "I highly doubt it, but it sure ain't anything normal either."

Ray stood over the beast's corpse. The crowd around him continued to grow. With David dead and Earl injured, everyone was looking to him for answers and what to do.

"Look," he told them, "It's all over. Everybody go back to your wagons. We'll get all this sorted out in the morning when we're thinking more clearly."

"No," Rain said as she stepped from the crowd. "Nothing is over. Proof lies at your feet and yet you still refuse to believe!"

"Rain!" Ray pleaded with her, "This isn't the time."

"There may be no other time, Ray Warren. The beast's kin will be coming if they are not already here and watching us as we speak."

"You mean there's more of those things out there?" someone in the crowd whimpered.

"God help us," a woman muttered loud enough to be heard.

"We don't know anything for sure yet folks!" Ray shouted. "There's no reason to panic!"

A chorus of roars and shrieks erupted in the night from somewhere among the trees beyond the rear of the wagon train. A lone gunshot echoed and was followed by the sound of screams.

"Oh Lord, they're here!" someone wailed.

"Run!" a frazzled looking man who came darting up the row of wagons yelled at the crowd. The crowd split apart, folks running every which way. Some raced for their wagons while others took off blindly into the woods. Ray leapt forward grabbing Rain by her arm. She winced from the pressure of his grip.

"You've just killed us all," Ray snarled at her. "Together we might have had a prayer," Ray waved a hand at the chaos around them now, "but like this... they'll get us one by one."

"Ray!" Bentley shouted. The Irish man was dragging a heavy looking box down the line of wagons towards them. "You're going to need this!"

Several guns could be heard now from all along the length of the wagon train. The roars of the beasts, and the screams of the dying men and women the creatures were tearing into were louder and more constant than the sounds of those trying to fight back against them.

"What the Hell is that?" Ray asked as Bentley stopped where he was and started unlocking the box he had been dragging.

"It's what's going to keep us alive," Bentley

said proudly with a huge grin.

Ray knew the Irish man was an inventor but he couldn't believe what he saw as Bentley wrenched a strange gun like object from inside the box. The weapon was massive by normal standards. It had six, wide shotgun style barrels and two levers protruded from its underside. Three triggers sat in front of the two levers protected by a small, rifle type guard. Bentley was having trouble holding the gun, it looked like it was all the little Irish man could do to hold it up. He shoved it at Ray. "Take it. It's the world's first and only six barrel, combat shotgun."

Ray blinked, too stunned to move.

"Each of the levers loads three shells at a time. The first trigger on the right is single shot, one barrel fired per squeeze. The far left trigger fires three at once. The middle is the big boom. The gun holds twelve shells total, fully loaded, which it is."

Bentley pressed the monstrous weapon into Ray's hands. "I'm not a fighter. You are. Take it and get me out of here alive!" Bentley begged.

The gun was really heavy. Ray wondered how Bentley had lifted it at all as he took it and nearly dropped it before he changed his hold on it, shifting it around, Ray got accustomed to its weight. Rain had no gun but she had produced a long, lethal looking knife from God knew where and held it ready, her eyes watching for another of the beasts to show itself. Ray saw Darlene helping Earl to his feet.

He rushed over to help them, Rain and Bentley following him.

"Make for the lead wagon!" Ray ordered.

The beasts were everywhere. They came at the wagons from all sides, bursting from the trees into the mass of panicked travelers. John Watkins watched as one of the monsters slammed into his wagon, splintering the wood of its side, and flung it over with Grace still inside of it. Angie was running for the wagon as it flipped over onto her.

"Angie!" John yelled as the beasts jumped onto the wagons' bottom, pressing it downwards further onto both his wife and daughter as it sprang towards him. John knew they were both dead, crushed beneath the weight of wood and muscle. He jerked the butt of his Winchester to his shoulder, taking aim at the beast's throat. Pastor Page grabbed him as he squeezed the trigger. His shot flew over the monster's head into the darkness beyond the trail.

"No!" Pastor Page shouted. "We need to make a run for it! We can't win this fight."

John tore free of the pastor's grip. "Suit yourself pastor!" John said, tears sliding over his cheeks and burning his eyes. "I'm staying right here!"

John worked the rifle's lever, chambering a fresh round as Pastor Page disappeared into the trees. John looked up into gleaming yellow eyes and saw that the beast had reached him. Its fingers closed over the Winchester's barrel, bending and twisting the metal with the pressure of its grip. John let go of the rifle and went for the pistol holstered on his belt. The beast was faster though. A swing of its left hand took John's head from his shoulders in an explosion of blood and sent it bouncing across the trail.

Jocie clutched Vincent's wrist tightly as she dragged him along behind her. The two children sprinted up the line of wagons towards Earl's where they hoped their mother would be. Jocie could hear her crying out to them from somewhere near the head of the wagon train. They had to reach her. Jocie wasn't ready to die and as annoying as he was, Vincent didn't deserve to either. Her little brother was in tears and the front of his pants was darkened by a wet patch where he had pissed himself as they ran.

"Mom!" Jocie called out. "We're coming! Hold on!"

All around them, folks were dying. A man with two Colts stepped into their path. He was firing into the woods on the right side of the trail, both guns spitting lead, over and over. One of the monsters ran straight into him like a runaway train, splattering them with his blood as it carried him on with it, out of their path. Jocie scooped Vincent up, carrying him in her arms, and pushed herself onward at an even faster pace. Her breath came in ragged gasps and her legs felt as if they were on fire. Pain blossomed in her chest and her vision blurred, but still she ran towards her mother's voice through a gauntlet of horrors. A beast squatted over a gutted woman, shoving handfuls of her entrails into its blood smeared mouth to the sound of smacking lips. Jocie saw one man bury the blade of an axe into the stomach of one of the monsters before it reached out and bent his top half over backwards to touch the backsides of his legs. The cracking noise of his breaking spine was loud and clear even over the man's final scream. Another of the beasts held a struggling woman in its arm. It ripped open the front of her blue dress and buried its head in her bouncing breasts. Jocie couldn't tell if the creature was raping the woman or eating her. Either way, there was nothing she could do to help. Reaching their mother, Darlene, was all that mattered.

Ray and his small group of followers had reached the lead wagon. They waited for Darlene's kids to catch up to them as Bentley worked to get the horses loose from their harnesses. Ray's own horse was gone.

"Forget it!" Earl shouted at Bentley. "Leave them horses be!"

"We can't use the wagon!" Bentley argued.

"The trail is too..."

"Get in!" Ray grabbed Bentley and dragged him around to shove him into the wagon's rear. "You able to drive it?" He asked Earl as he turned around.

"I reckon I don't have a choice," Earl let Darlene help him up onto the driver's seat. The kids made it to them. Darlene ran to them, hugging them both at once as Ray watched. They hopped into the wagon's rear with Bentley as one of the monsters came at the group. Rain kept by Ray's side as he shouldered the six barrel and let it rip. He waited until the beast was so close its stench made him gag before he squeezed the middle trigger. All six barrels thundered in an orange explosion of fire and death. The six slugs blew a gaping hole through the monster reducing the thing's chest to nothing more than a mangled mess of dripping meat. The monster thudded to the dirt and lay still. The recoil nearly shattered Ray's shoulder. He stumbled, barely managing to stay on his feet and keep his hold on the weapon. "Mother..." he swore, rubbing at his bruised shoulder.

"Sorry about that," Ray heard Bentley yell. "Forgot to warn you, it has got kind of a kick to it."

"Dang it, Bentley!" he worked both of the levers at once, reloading all six bars with one motion.

"We must go, Ray Warren," Rain told him.

Ray nodded at her. " I know, I know."

Together they climbed into the wagon as

Earl whipped the horses into an outright sprint. The animals strained against their harnesses as the wagon bounced and jerked up the trail behind them.

Pastor Page watched the last of his fellow travelers die from on high. He had climbed to the top of a tree and was perched on one of its upper branches. So far, none of the monsters had noticed him. They were too busy venting their anger upon the corpses of those they had just killed and smashing the wagons to pieces. Never would he have believed such beasts could be real. There was nothing in the good book about them. Like men though, they were also God's creations, but Pastor Page couldn't begin to imagine why the Lord would breathe life into things like them. It wasn't his place however to figure out the Lord's plan, but to serve him in all things with his heart. If the Lord willed that he die here tonight at the hands and claws of these beasts, then so be it. Pastor Page whispered a prayer for the dead below. When he opened his eyes and looked down, a sea of blood smeared, hate filled faces stared up at him. Over a dozen of the beasts had gathered around the bottom of the tree and he knew his fate was sealed.

✶ ✶ ✶

Snell had chosen to keep ridding on through the night. He wanted to be sure there was no chance of Bentley escaping him. Catching Bentley on the trail known as Devil's Pass would be his last hope of doing so before the wagon train reached the West and Bentley would be able to vanish, possibly forever, into the crowds of the homesteaders, traders, and boom towns. Snell's eyes were sharp. He spotted the Indians coming from quite a ways off. There were five of them, all armed, all warriors from the looks of them. War paint was smeared over their faces. Scalps bounced on the sides of their hips as they rode towards him. They were moving at a normal pace and it looked as if they planned to meet him, not run him down. Snell sighed. The Indians were just one more obstacle between him and his prey. He pulled up his horse and stopped to wait on them. They approached him slowly, weapons out and ready, but not in an overly threatening manner, more in the manner of a subtle warning. The lead Indian said "hello" in the language of the Apache and raised his hand. The others watched Snell closely, ready to gun him down at the first sign of danger.

"I got no quarrel with you," Snell told them. "Let me pass and there doesn't have to be blood split here tonight."

The lead Indian shook his head in the

negative and spouted a long string of words that Snell didn't understand. He got the sense that they were trying to warn him away from something that lay up ahead. Well, they could forget that. He had to go this way and they could be damned if they stood in his way.

"Move aside boys," Snell snarled, the impatience clear on his face, "Or I am going through you. Understand?"

The Indians made no motion to clear the path. The one that appeared to be their leader continued to wave a hand at him and point back the way he'd come. "Sasquatch!" the Indian said louder. "You go or die. If you die, they perhaps come for us too." The last bit was in poor, jagged English, but Snell was able to make it out.

Snell looked from one Indian's face to the next. He could see that they weren't about to back down without a fight. "Too bad fellas," he whispered.

One of Snell's Colts left its holster in a blur. Three of the Indians were dead before they could even move. He'd started with the one on the far right and put a bullet into each as he moved the barrel of the gun across the length of their party. The fourth Indian tried to dodge but instead ended up catching a round in his shoulder that threw him from his saddle. The last Indian came charging towards Snell with a tomahawk in his hand and a war cry on his lips. Snell spurred his horse forward, dropping his pistol and drawing the small sword strapped to his back. His blade met the

Indian's hand sending it and the tomahawk spinning away into the darkness with a single swipe. Snell's backswing caught the warrior across his face, slashing open his cheek in a second spray of blood as the Indian screamed and toppled from his horse to the ground. The Indian with the wounded shoulder had somehow managed to reclaim his rifle and held it aimed at Snell. Snell ducked in his saddle as the rifle cracked and a bullet whizzed over his head. Snell drew his other Colt and fired three times. Each bullet smashed into the Indian's head making a mess of his face and leaving his corpse twitching in the grass. Snell whirled to see the last Indian clutching at the bleeding stub of his right hand as he tried to run away. A single shot from Snell's Colt dropped him, burying itself into the Indian's spine. Snell holstered his Colt and removed a piece of cloth from his pocket. He wiped his blade clean of blood and sheathed it in the scabbard he wore on his back. Snell spat on the closest of the bodies. Stupid savages, he thought. He dismounted and retrieved his other Colt then got back in the saddle. He rode on into the night towards the Devil's Pass as if nothing had happened, his thoughts once again solely concerned with what waited for him there.

The wagon didn't make it far before it was

too busted up to keep moving. Ray and the others abandoned it and kept moving on foot. There was no sign of the beasts, but Ray wasn't so dumb as to think they had lost the monsters. Earl wasn't holding up much better than the wagon had. Sweat slicked his hair and skin. A thin strand of blood leaked from the right corner of his mouth. Each of the big man's breath was a rattling wheeze. If they didn't stop moving soon Earl was a goner. Hell, he bloody was already, Ray admitted to himself. Earl was as dead as those they had left behind with the beasts, everyone was just pretending he wasn't as if they refused to accept that it was only a matter of time. Besides, Ray couldn't let them stop. As long as they were alive, there was hope, and they needed to put as much distance between themselves and the beasts as they could. Making a stand wasn't an option. Ray figured there were at least two dozen of the beasts, and the group was in no shape to handle more than one of them... even that much was questionable. Bentley didn't have any extra shells for the six barrel. When the barrels were empty this time, they would stay that way.

"Anybody got a plan?" Ray asked as the group continued limping along at the best pace they could muster. Bentley shook his head sadly.

"There will be no escape. None of us will see the dawn," Rain told them. "The question is how will we face our death when it comes."

"Shut up," Ray snapped at the Indian

woman. "I have had quite enough of your demon talk. You watched me kill one of those things. They're not supernatural. We can out think them. They're just animals, even if they do walk on two legs."

Earl broke into a coughing fit that ended in tears of pain and hacking up a mouthful of blood. "I got a plan," the big man rasped. "You folks leave me that there gun with the six barrels and keep going. I'll hold those hairy sons of bitches here."

"Not gonna happen," Ray said firmly.

"Come on, Ray. I'm dead either way and we both know it. No use in dragging me along. Only gonna slow you down more," Earl argued. "Let me die like a man, not a cripple."

"You wouldn't even slow them down, Earl, six barrel or not, and I ain't about to hand over the only real weapon we got to be left behind."

Darlene still had her double barrel and both Bentley and Earl carried Colts in holsters on their hips, but without a lucky shot, all of them were next to useless against the beasts. The things' muscles were too dense for anything but the prototype's huge blast or concentrated fire to take down. And the beasts weren't going to be giving them a chance for anything like that, even if they had the ammo to pull it off, which they didn't.

"I'm sorry, Earl, but we have to keep going... all of us," Ray added after a second. "Maybe the things will get tired of chasing us and go away when the sun comes up."

"I wouldn't count on that," Bentley laughed

darkly. "From what our Indian friend here has told us," the Irish man gestured at Rain, "These things are highly territorial. They're not going to leave off until either we're all dead or far outside of their domain."

Ray sighed. "Am I the only one who hasn't given up already?"

"No sir," a timid voice answered him. It belonged to Darlene's daughter, Jocie. The girl pointed up through the trees to the northwest. "Why don't we hole up in there?"

Everyone went silent as they saw the cabin Jocie had spotted.

"A cabin, out here?" Earl coughed. "That don't make any sense."

Ray grinned. "Don't matter. It's an answer to our prayers. Come on folks. We got ourselves somewhere real to go now."

The cabin was old, and vines crept up its sides like green tendrils reaching for the sun. Its walls were battered by age and the elements, but still looked strong enough to do. The place had been extremely well built. Ray led the rest of the group inside.

"So who do you think built this place?" Bentley asked.

"I would wager this place belonged to a hunter or maybe a trapper," Ray said. "Look around. It wasn't a home, but a short term place to stay, maybe for a season." Ray turned to Rain. "These woods haven't always belonged to those monsters have they?"

"No," Rain answered, sheathing her knife and plopping onto the edge of the cabin's bed where it was shoved up against the rear wall. The only other piece of furniture was a large table in the cabin's center. It looked to have been a work table of some sort, perhaps for gutting and preparing whatever whoever had lived here had hunted. Dark stains marred its top. "Once the beasts roamed the whole land according to our legends," Rain continued, "Only in the last few decades have they withdrawn from the land and gathered here."

"Bentley, help me find a way to secure the door," Ray barked. "Everybody else, get some rest. One way or another, you're gonna need it when those things out there find us."

As the sun rose over Devil's Pass, Snell walked his horse along the rough trail through the woods. The air stunk of death and rot long before he found the reason why. What he discovered left him both baffled and keenly on guard. The wagon train, or rather what remained of it, was strewn about the trail in front of him. Very few of the corpses littering the trail were intact enough to truly be called such. Gnawed upon arms and legs, caved in and torn off heads, and other assorted bits of people lay everywhere. Most of the wagons themselves were little more than splintered piles of crushed and crumpled wood. Shredded clothes, bent guns, and other luggage were mixed in with the carnage as if whatever had done this had torn apart the people's belongings after the massacre. One of the more disturbing things however was half of a horse that hung five feet above the ground where it was impaled on the limb of a nearby tree. The branch completely pierced its upper body and its hind legs were gone. In their place was a mass of dangling red slicked intestines that touched the grass below it. Whatever had struck these folks had been brutal, fast, and ferocious. Despite the spent bullet casing and shells that lay here and there among the blades of the tall grass, Snell saw no signs of any causalities other than the folks of the wagon train itself. If any of the attackers had been killed, the surviving ones had carried off their dead with them when they had left the scene and returned to wherever they had come from. For all his experience with war and murder, Snell had never encountered anything remotely like what he saw here. Snell moved among the carnage inspecting the scene more closely. As he did so, he noticed the footprints. The prints had the general shape of a man's barefoot, but they were impossibly large and too deep to have been made by a human. By the depth of the indentions in the earth, Snell guessed the average weight of the attackers was somewhere close to one thousand pounds, if not more. His eyes bugged and he let out a long, low whistle in amazement. Snell counted twenty seven distinct sets of the tracks. One of the creatures that made them had to be wounded as one of the sets of tracks was staggered and marred as if whatever made it was dragging one of its feet. He found signs to confirm his suspicion that the attackers had indeed carried off their dead. Snell found himself longing for a bigger gun than those he had brought along for this job. He had brought a Winchester, a double barrel shotgun, and three pistols, counting the concealed one in his gear, between the weapons he carried and those stored away on his saddle with plenty of ammo for each of them but nothing that was beyond what the members of the wagon train would have used to defend themselves with... and clearly, it would not be enough. Snell unsung the Winchester strapped to his back and tucked it away in a holster on the side of his saddle opposite the double barrel, trading the rifle for his sword. He unsheathed the small, oriental blade and tested its sharpness. If he did run across one of the animals or creatures that had been responsible for the massacre here, he figured it was his best shot at slaying it. Snell had a passion for blades, though his work usually required bullets, and spent the better part of a decade, during his free time, becoming a master of the weapon he now held. He spun the small sword with his fingers, slicing the air once before returning it to its sheath. Though it was hard to tell from the mangled mess the wagon train's dead were in, Snell found nothing to prove that Bentley was among them. An empty case marked "property of the U.S. Army" lay open on the trail. Odds were the

Irish man had been forced to reveal and use the stolen weapon in order to stay alive during the course of the battle here.

Snell walked back to his horse and climbed onto its saddle. The animal was uneasy from something it smelt on the air and resisted his efforts to force it on deeper into the woods along the trail, but in the end discipline overcame its fear. Snell rode slowly onward in pursuit of his prey.

✶ ✶ ✶

Rain awoke, startled to be alive and breathing. She had been sure the beasts would come for them during the night. She glanced around the small room of the cabin. The others were asleep, except for the woman, Darlene. Even Ray, who sat with his back against the door and the six barreled weapon Bentley had given him across his lap, snored with his head sunk to his chest. Darlene cradled the big man named Earl's head. Her eyes were red from tears. It was clear to Rain that Earl was no longer with them. His soul must have moved on to the next life during the passage of the night. Rain sat up, stretching her arms above her head. "It was a good death," she told Darlene, "He died fighting to save those he cared for."

Darlene's body shook with fresh sobs as Ray stirred.

"What is it?" he asked them, then went silent as he saw Darlene and realized what had happened. Ray got to his feet. "Wake the others," he ordered Rain. "We need to get moving."

Rain stared at him. "Do you honestly believe we can reach the other side of the pass and make it out of these woods alive?" She saw in his face that he did not even as he answered her.

"We have to try. I ain't never been a quitter and I don't plan on starting. Besides, if I am gonna die, I would rather go out swinging than cowering in this cabin waiting on death to come to me."

Darlene's children were already up, awakened by their voices. They sat quietly, watching their mother, full of fear and appearing unsure as to what to do.

Rain stood and walked over to where Bentley lay curled up in a ball on the floor. She nudged him with her foot. "Get up Irish man. It's time to go."

Groggily, Bentley rolled onto his back looking up at her. "Go where my dear? We are in the heart of the beasts' domain if your legends are true. There is nowhere we can go and not encounter them. They will surely still be hunting for us, even now."

Ray stormed over and yanked Bentley to his feet. "You shut up that kind of talk this instant. We got children with us."

The Irish man craned his neck to glance at Jocie and Vincent. "You would rather lie to them? Give them hope when there isn't any?"

Rain saw something break in Ray. His features became an expression of absolute rage as he planted a fist in the dainty Irish man's stomach. Bentley's breath left his lungs in an explosive grunt before he collapsed to the wooden floor of the cabin on his hands and knees in front of Ray.

"Your gun may have saved us sir," Ray growled, towering over him, "but I'll be damned if I'm gonna let you put these children through more than they have to face."

Ray spun leaving Bentley on his knees, gasping for breath, to face her as Rain watched him. "You know about these creatures. Is there anything we can do to make peace with them somehow?"

Though Ray's anger frightened her, she told him the truth, not what he wanted to hear. "Die," she said simply in the calmest voice she could manage.

Ray started to backhand her, but he caught himself at the last moment. Rain didn't flinch as he did it. She had been struck before and by far less gentle men than Ray was in his heart despite his gruff exterior. One had to merely look into his eyes and you could see the goodness he fought so hard to suppress within them. She understood how he must feel now. The lives of everyone in this cabin rested on his shoulders and his task was an impossible one. After a moment, she said, "Not as many of the beasts will be about during the day. They will have stuffed themselves last night and they did not come for us as I believed they would. Perhaps there is some hope of us escaping these woods if we can do it before night falls again."

"All right then," Ray said, "You heard the lady. Everyone up and on your feet. We need to get moving."

"What about Earl?" Darlene asked sadly.

"I'm sorry, Darlene," Ray shook his head. "We don't have time to bury him and we sure can't haul his body with us."

With everyone as ready as they could be, Rain watched Ray carefully crack the door to look outside.

"It's clear as best I can tell," he said. Ray opened the door the rest of the way to take a step forward as a rifle cracked from somewhere among the trees. The bullet ripped through his heart and burst from his back in an explosion of red wetness and tiny bone fragments that splashed onto those closest to him. Jocie cried out as his blood rained over her. Ray was dead before his body hit the floor.

"Get down!" Rain yelled as the cabin door swung even further open. There was no second shot. Instead, a cold, gravelly voice called out, "There a man named Bentley in there?"

Rain looked at the Irish man. Bentley had gone pale as if he recognized the voice and would have rather had the beasts waiting outside. The six barreled shotgun lay near Ray's body in a pool of still warm blood. Rain knew she would never reach it even if she tried for the weapon. The man outside would put a bullet in her skull before she ever had a chance to use it. Darlene gestured at her, catching her attention, and tossed her Earl's pistol. Rain caught it and was glad to feel its weight on her palm. Bentley was so scared he looked on the verge of being sick.

"Who's out there?" Rain demanded.

"His name is Snell," Bentley whispered. "He's a bounty hunter."

"You're a wanted man?" Darlene asked in utter shock. "What in the devil did you do?"

Bentley rubbed at his cheeks with his fingers. "I took back something that was mine."

Rain leveled the barrel of Earl's pistol at him and pulled its hammer back. "Need some more explaining than that."

"I build things, create them. I made that gun there for the army," Bentley pointed at the six barrel. "They commissioned it, but they decided it was too unwieldy and hard to reload to be of use on the battlefield. They were going to destroy it. I couldn't let that happen. Said they couldn't risk its design getting out in case someone else could improve on it and make it more functional... But it's my baby. I couldn't sit back and let them do that. I worked too hard on making it a reality."

"And now a good man is lying dead because of it," Rain snarled at the Irish man, "Is this Snell after you or the gun?"

"I don't know," Bentley wailed. "Honestly, I don't. He could want me and it. They know I can build another one given the time and the resources."

"So even if we give him the gun..."

"He will kill us all," Bentley finished for her.

"You bastard," Darlene yelled at him.

"I didn't... I didn't think he would ever be able to find me," Bentley sobbed, but Rain only half heard his words. She was trying to get a better look outside from where she stood without making herself a target. They hadn't answered the bounty hunter's call and he'd been quiet out there for too long to be up to anything but trouble. Snell couldn't possibly know how many of them were in the cabin or how well armed they might be. Rain tried to think on what she would do next in his position.

A whiskey bottle came flying into the cabin. A flaming piece of rag stuck out of its neck. It landed on the floor near Darlene and her children where they huddled together, shattering in an explosion of burning liquid. Before Rain could even move, Darlene and the children were on fire. The flames quickly spread across the floor and up the walls. The ancient and weathered wood of the cabin caught and added to the growing mass of flame and heat. There was nothing Rain could do as she listened to them screaming. She saw Darlene, ignoring the flames on her flesh and clothes, as the woman tried to save Jocie and Vincent, but it was hopeless as a second bottle came whirling through the open door and burst near where the first had. The heat, smoke, and smell of cooking meat was unbearable.

Bentley made no move to help the others. Instead, the Irish man darted into the light of the sun outside leaving them all to burn. Rain followed after him, keeping him between her and the woods facing the doorway. A rifle cracked just as she had known it would. Bentley's right knee disintegrated under him as he shrieked in pain and went tumbling into the grass. Rain flung herself to the ground as the rifle cracked again. She felt a bullet graze her hair as she hit the dirt. She blindly returned fire with the pistol she carried, popping off several rounds in the direction the shot had come from.

"Toss the gun away or you're dead," Snell shouted. He was close but Rain didn't dare try to take a chance at spotting him. Rain threw her revolver towards the trees. Bentley was writhing around in agony, clutching what remained of his knee. She felt no pity for the Irish man as he wailed and tears rolled over his cheeks. Any man who would leave a mother and her children to die such a gruesome death wasn't worth the effort. Of course, she hadn't tried either, but she chose not to dwell on that. The family had died the moment the first bottle struck the cabin's floor. That was just the truth of the matter. Rain lay still, at Snell's mercy, waiting on the bounty hunter to make the next move. Snell came swaggering from the trees, a wide grin spreading his lips. His rifle was slung over his back alongside some kind of strange sword sheathed there, its hilt extending in easy reach above his left shoulder. An expensive, custom designed Colt was in his hand. He kept the pistol aimed at her as he walked toward Bentley. The Irish man stared at Snell with wide, wet eyes.

"Where is it?" Snell demanded.

Bentley released his grip on the bleeding remnants of his knee long enough to point at the smoldering cabin. The whole building was now a raging inferno. Black smoke rose into the sky above it. "It's in there you bastard," Bentley said through clenched teeth. "Go on and get it if you want."

Snell stared at the cabin. "Damn," the bounty hunter muttered just loud enough to be heard. Rain saw the anger rising within him.

"You little yellow bellied prick." Snell stepped on Bentley's wounded knee, grinding it against the dirt with the heel of one of his heavy boots. Bentley howled from the pain, grabbing a hold of Snell's leg to try to make the bounty hunter stop. Snell lowered the barrel of his pistol and put a bullet, point blank, into the Irish man's forehead. The backside of Bentley's skull blew outward. Brain matter splattered on the grass in glistening, red smeared gray clumps. Bentley's twitching form slumped over. Snell kicked Bentley's dead hands off of the leg of his pants and turned to her.

"Well girl, this didn't exactly go as I planned," he laughed darkly.

Rain had gotten up on her knees. She froze and remained silent. Snell shook his head.

"Didn't figure on the Irish man being dumb enough to let the gun burn after all he went through to keep it." Snell spat on Bentley's corpse. "Dang fool."

"We're not safe here," Rain worked up the nerve to say.

"I saw what happened to the wagons," Snell said. "You want to tell me what on God's earth the things were that did that to those folks?"

"The smell of cooking meat and blood will draw them here," Rain warned him again. "We must leave now."

But she saw it was already too late.

The beasts emerged from the trees around the cabin, encircling them where they stood. There was nowhere to run. There were nine of the monsters in all. In the center of their ranks, behind Snell was what had to be their chief. While all of the beasts were massive and incredibly tall, it towered over the others and the bounty hunter, a good twelve feet of thick muscle and unbridled rage. She saw Snell shrug and drop his pistol.

"Girl, I guess the fun we were about to have is gonna have to wait," he told her.

She felt more than his eyes roam over the curves of her body, then with a sigh he reached for the hilt of his sword. The instant his fingers closed on it, Snell spun, leaping at the twelve foot tall beast as he drew it. His blade sliced through the monster's throat. The beast gave a gargled cry of surprise that he'd managed to hurt it as blood exploded from the wound and flowed down over the brown hair of its chest. Snell struck it twice more, slashing a deep gash along its inner thigh, then again, batting away one of its reaching hands, taking two of its fingers in the process. Snell's movements were like a dance as he side stepped the beast's toppling corpse and let it fall to the dirt to bleed out.

With a chorus of roars the other beasts sprang forward. Snell met one with a swipe that took away half its face. Snell hopped backwards, spinning to catch another of the beasts across its eyes with his blade. The beast shrieked, blinded, covering its butchered, empty sockets with large, hairy hands. Snell ducked under and through the snatching claws of two more of the creatures and came up burying his blade into another's groin. The beast's manhood flopped to the ground between its legs as its eyes went wide and it cried out in a high pitched voice filled with fear and pain. Three of the beasts came at Rain as she leapt to her feet. The last she saw of Snell as she fled into the trees was the beasts' sheer numbers finally overwhelming the bounty hunter. As he slashed the chest of one monster, another scooped him up from behind, enveloping him in its thick arms. Rain heard Snell's screams behind her as she ran. Her legs pumped beneath her as she poured on every ounce of speed she could muster. It wasn't enough. She felt long, wide fingers grasp her hair as the first one of the monsters chasing her got within reach. It yanked on her hair, snapping her head back, and sending her feet flying out from under her. She landed hard on her back, her breath leaving her body.

In the next second, they were all on her. She tried to scream as hairy hands ripped her breeches from her legs, but there was no air left in her lungs. A hairy finger plunged into her open mouth as one the beasts took hold of her by her chin. The creature slammed her head into the dirt and then there was only blackness and distant pain.

The End

About The Author

Eric S. Brown is the author of numerous books including the **"Bigfoot War"** series, the **"A Pack of Wolves"** series, **"War of the Worlds Plus Blood Guts and Zombies"**, **"World War of the Dead"**, **"Season of Rot"**, **"Last Stand in a Dead Land"**, and **"The Weaponer"** to name only a few. He lives in North Carolina with his family where he continues to write tales of blazing guns, the hungry dead, and the things that lurk in the woods.

Visit his website at
http://ericsbrown.wordpress.com

From the mind of Eric S. Brown,
Coscom Entertainment proudly presents…

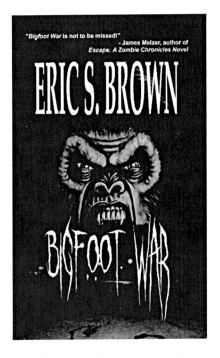

The town of Babble Creek is about to find out Bigfoot
is very real and there's more than one of the creatures
that want to fill the streets with blood.

"BIGFOOT WAR is not to be missed!"
- James Melzer, author of ESCAPE: A ZOMBIE
CHRONICLES NOVEL

Available at Your Favorite Online Retailer or Through Your Local Bookstore.

ISBN: 970-1-926712-49-9
www.coscomentertainment.com

CPSIA information can be obtained
at www.ICGtesting.com
Printed in the USA
FFOW04n0801151215
19678FF